# HANNAH AND DARJEELING

Moving to a new neighbourhood can be a difficult time – but it can also be a lot of fun, as Hannah discovers!

Diana Hendry is the author of numerous stories for young readers, such as *Fiona Finds Her Tongue* (shortlisted for the Smarties Prize), *Midnight Pirate, Hetty's First Fling, Kid Kibble* (1992) and another Walker Double – *The Dream Camel and the Dazzling Cat*. She has also written two novels – *Double Vision*, for young adults and *Harvey Angell*, winner of the 1991 Whitbread Children's Novel Award. In her spare time she enjoys wearing interesting hats and spinning plates! She lives in Bristol with her son, daughter and piano.

# HANNAH
## AND
# DARJEELING

## DIANA HENDRY

Illustrated by
Mei-Yim Low

WALKER BOOKS
LONDON

For Hamish
*(The Not-Anywhere House)*

For my mother
*(The Rainbow Watchers)*

First published 1989 by Julia MacRae Books
as *The Not-Anywhere House* and *The Rainbow Watchers*

This edition published 1992 by
Walker Books Ltd, 87 Vauxhall Walk
London SE11 5HJ

Text © 1989 Diana Hendry
Illustrations © 1989 Mei-Yim Low
Cover illustration © 1992 Virginia Chalcraft

Printed and bound in Great Britain by
Richard Clay Ltd, Bungay, Suffolk

British Library Cataloguing in Publication Data
A catalogue record for this title is available
from the British Library.
ISBN 0-7445-2303-6

# CONTENTS

## The Not-Anywhere House

## The Rainbow Watchers

# THE NOT-ANYWHERE HOUSE
## Chapter 1

The new house wasn't new at all. It was an old house right in the middle of the city. The houses in Totterdown Street looked like people on a tube train in the rush hour, all squashed together and trying to make themselves as skinny as possible. Number 325, Hannah's house, was four storeys high and Hannah's room was to be at the very top, in the attic.

"You'll be like a bird in a nest at the top of a tree," said Hannah's father.

"I like *this* nest," said Hannah who was sitting on her bean bag in her bedroom at Dungee Farm Cottage, Loose End. Darjeeling the cat sat next to her. Darjeeling folded his paws into a muff, rested his chin and shut his eyes.

"Darjeeling is saying his prayers," said Hannah. "He doesn't want to move either."

Dungee Farm Cottage had been home to Hannah for as long as she could remember. The village, with its six cottages, one pub and one post-office-that-sold-everything, was the only place she knew.

But Mr Knap had found a job in the city. He had been looking for a job for a long time. "I can't miss this one," he said, "and it's too far to travel. I'd never be home in time to read you a bed-time story, Hannah. We have to move."

Hannah's mother said that Loose End was a dump anyway. "It's at the end of everything," she said. "There are no shops, no cinemas, no library, no theatre, no nothing.

The city will be fun."

But Hannah liked the 'nothing'
that stretched beyond Dungee Farm
Cottage, in field after field after
field until it melted into sky. It
made you think that although there
was an end to Loose End (on the
corner by the post-box), there was
no end to the world.

Most of all, Hannah liked the
willow tree that grew outside her
bedroom window. The willow, with
its long pale fronds, reminded

Hannah of her cousin, Lucy. Lucy was sixteen and had long fair hair which she was always washing, but which she never combed or cut. The willow tree had hair like that, newly washed every morning, and in the wind it shifted and shuffled its fronds and seemed to be whispering secrets about growing up and having long hair that you never combed. Hannah called it the talking tree.

"You'll have a splendid view

from your new bedroom window," said Hannah's father. "You'll be able to see all the lights of the city and all the spires of the churches."

"But no talking tree," said Hannah, taking Darjeeling into her lap. "Darjeeling is a country cat," she said, "he likes the dark fields at night. He likes being all slinky. That's why he's black. He won't like the city lights."

"He'll enjoy exploring all the gardens in Totterdown Street," said Mrs Knap, "and climbing over walls and meeting other cats. Now why don't you and Darjeeling go out into the garden because I have a lot of boxes to pack."

The boxes had been delivered that morning. They came as flat squares of cardboard and had to be made into boxes. Lined up in the sitting room, the flat squares looked like a giant's brown sliced loaf. Hannah's father was packing books. All the friendly things from the shelf in the kitchen — the brown milk jug, the small spotted sugar bowl, the red coffee pot and the

little tubs of herbs and spices with
their neat labels saying, 'ginger',
'rosemary', 'parsley', 'peppercorn'
— had already been put away.

Hannah carried Darjeeling out
into the garden. She sat on the
swing and talked to the willow tree.

"We're leaving you, tree," said
Hannah, "and someone else is
coming to look after you, only I
don't know if they speak tree

language." The willow shook and shivered. "I can't take you with me," continued Hannah, "because you belong here. You've got roots, you see, and they won't come out."

"You've got roots here, too, Hannah," said her father, coming to the kitchen door. "They go down at least six years. But I think we can plant you again in Totterdown Street. In my opinion little girls are like poppies, they'll grow anywhere."

"I don't think I'll grow anywhere else but Loose End," said Hannah.

"I'm sure you will," said her father. "I'll give you a nice mulchy compost for breakfast instead of cornflakes. By next spring you'll have grown at least three inches. You might even be a cherry blossom if you cheer up."

"I won't," said Hannah. "I'll be a weeping willow with long tossy hair."

"I'd rather you were a happy willow with long tossy hair," said Mr Knap. (Hannah's hair was short and dark and frizzy.) "Come on, let's go and take a cutting from the red rose and another from the yellow rose and then tomorrow we can plant them in the new garden."

So Hannah went and found the secateurs from the garden shed and her father took a cutting from each rose tree and put them inside a polythene bag to keep them warm.

"There!" he said. "That's one scarlet *Ena Harkness* and one yellow *Angela* and one darkly delicious Hannah — all to be replanted tomorrow."

Tomorrow was moving day. By night-time everything was looking very strange in Dungee Farm Cottage. The lamp shades were down and the bare light bulbs shone into all the empty corners. Their coats were off the hooks in the hall and piled up on a chair, ready. The pictures had been packed so that you could just see grey squares on the walls where pictures had been.

"Perhaps I'll leave my shadow behind," said Hannah, "so people will know where I have been."

"We can't possibly go without your shadow," said Hannah's father. "But I'm sure there's something of you that will stay behind here. Let's find a floorboard and we can scratch your name on it."

So they went up to Hannah's

bedroom and found a corner where no-one would mind someone writing their name, and Hannah's father gave her his penknife and Hannah scratched her name out very slowly and carefully because it was difficult enough with a pencil and much more difficult with a knife and because 'H' is a very difficult letter to do with a knife. The letters came out all squiffy, like this

HANNAH

Then Hannah's father scratched the year very neatly after her name, and Hannah added a kiss because she thought the next people might like one.

# Chapter 2

In the morning Darjeeling was packed into a box. But it was a special cat box with holes in it so that Darjeeling could breathe, and had a blanket at the bottom so that he was cosy. Darjeeling pressed his quivering wet nose against one of the holes and miaowed.

"It's to keep him safe," explained Hannah's father. "Cats don't like moving. I don't want Darjeeling to run away."

"I think my voice has run away," said Hannah, because with

everything packed up, Dungee
Farm Cottage sounded very hollow
and their voices echoed.

"You *and* your voice, *and* your
shadow, *and* Darjeeling, are all
coming to Totterdown Street," said
Hannah's mother. "Now come and
help me make some sandwiches
because we'll be far too busy
unpacking to cook a proper meal."

So Hannah went into the kitchen (which was looking very unhomely without the mugs on the hooks and Darjeeling's red and blue bowls in their proper places by the back door) and helped to make a lot of sandwiches and a big flask of coffee and a bottle of blackcurrant for herself. And she began to feel more cheerful because it felt like going on a picnic or going on holiday.

At ten o'clock the Removal Men came in a van as big as a whale. There were three men. One was tall and thin, one was round and fat and the third was only a lad. They wore aprons with pockets round their waists and inside the pockets

were tools — hammers and
screwdrivers — for taking beds and
tables apart and putting them
together again.

The van-as-big-as-a-whale opened
its mouth and the Removal Men fed
it with cupboards and chairs, tables
and teapots, beds, brooms, buckets
and baskets, pots and pans and
even the piano which was put on a
special trolley and wheeled into the

Whale like a hospital patient on a stretcher. The Whale-Van was so big that the furniture seemed to shrink and looked no bigger than dolls' house furniture.

The Removal Men worked very quickly. They got cupboards out of tight spots, they made beds bend round corners, they persuaded wardrobes through doorways that were too small for them.

Very soon Dungee Farm Cottage was completely empty. It looked like an orphan, unloved and lonely. Hannah sat on the kitchen floor and cried all over Darjeeling's box and Darjeeling, who had fallen asleep, woke up and huffed and puffed

inside the box and scratched to
come out.

"The house is empty of us, too,"
sobbed Hannah, "we've been
poured away like a bucket of water
down the sink."

"What nonsense!" said Mr Knap.
(He was looking very fussed and red
in the face because one of the book
boxes had burst and the books had
fallen out in a jumble on the door-
step.) "Why, you'd block up all
the drains and I'd have to get

Dyno-Rod to hose you out, and out you'd come in a great whoosh!"

They re-packed the books in another box and carried it out to the Whale-Van. The Removal Men were having a tea-break. The round, fat man was trying out the piano and the lad was singing. He sang, "One Potato, Two Potato, Three Potato, Four."

Hannah and her father joined in. It felt like a street party.

After they'd sung to "Seven Potato More" three times, Hannah's father said, "Come on, let's go and say a proper goodbye to everything."

So they said goodbye to Hannah's bedroom window with the

hook that didn't hook properly, and
they said goodbye to the back door
with its great big key that didn't
turn properly, and they said
goodbye to the toy cupboard and
goodbye to the bath and goodbye to

the cupboard under the stairs and goodbye to the little brass doorknob and goodbye to the garden and, last of all, Hannah said goodbye to the willow tree.

She flung her arms around its trunk and gave it a good hug. "Goodbye, talking tree," she said, "I hope someone else will talk to you when I'm gone." And the tree shivered and shook all over and Hannah thought it whispered, "I wish you wouldn't go, I wish you wouldn't, I wish wish wish . . ."

"Goodbye old tree," said Hannah's father and then the three of them went back through the house and out of the front door of

Dungee Farm Cottage for the last time and got into the car.

"We've got to race the Removal Men to Totterdown Street," said Hannah's father. But it wasn't much of a race because the car was small and light and the Whale-Van was big and heavy and groaned up the hills away from Loose End.

Darjeeling, who hated car journeys, began to howl. Hannah started to cry again. (Darjeeling thought it was raining on his box.)

"The new house will soon feel like home," said Mrs Knap, finding a handkerchief that was not too clean and a cheering-up chocolate biscuit, "you wait and see."

# Chapter 3

But it didn't feel like home. The
houses of Totterdown Street
tottered down a steep hill. Old street
lamps leaned backwards to stop
themselves sliding to the bottom.
Telephone wires looped across the
street as if the houses on either side
were playing a game of cat's
cradle. And number 325 felt cold
and empty and strange.

Hannah had brought her duvet
with her in the car. She let it fall on
the floor like a gloomy cloud and
sat on it. The room didn't seem to

be any kind of room. It had a lot of
dust.

"This isn't anywhere," said
Hannah.

"Oh yes it is," said her mother,
bringing in a lamp which she loved
so dearly she had carried it herself.
"This is the sitting room." And she
set the lamp on the floor and
switched on the light.

The lamp made patterns on the
wall just as it had done at Dungee
Farm Cottage.

Mr Knap came in carrying the cat box and out jumped Darjeeling. A very fat Darjeeling. Crossness puffed him up. "Darling Darjeeling!" cried Hannah. "Come and have a cuddle." But Darjeeling took one startled look at the room that wasn't yet anywhere and fled up the stairs.

"Let him explore," said Hannah's father. "You come with me, Hannah, I've something to show you." And he marched Hannah out of the back door and into the garden.

There stood the tallest tree you ever did see. It was like a giant Christmas tree and it went on and

on and on and on. On past
Hannah's attic window, on towards
the sky. It was taller than the
house.

"It's a Monterey Pine," said
Hannah's father. "It comes from
California, America."

"What a long way to come," said
Hannah, looking up and up and
UP at the tree. "It looks as if it's
been here for ever."

"It probably thinks Totterdown Street is home now, just as you will one day," said her father.

"Do you think it's a talking tree?" asked Hannah. "It looks rather grand and snooty as if it wouldn't talk to anyone but the sun or the moon."

"Talk to it politely," said her father. "Making friends with trees and making friends with houses is something you can't rush."

Hannah looked up at the dark green branches of the Monterey Pine. "Good Afternoon Monterey Pine from California, America, The World," she said. "My name is Hannah and I'm very pleased to meet you."

But the tree said nothing and just then the Removal Men arrived in the Whale-Van. They opened up the Whale's mouth and there was all their furniture, safe and sound. Hannah's mother greeted each item like a long-lost friend.

The piano which had been last in was first out and was wheeled into the sitting room like a Very Important Person (which indeed it was) and Hannah's mother said, "Just there," and the Removal Men put the piano 'just there' — which was in the corner near the lamp.

Then everything started coming in very fast and all in the wrong order. The sofa came with the lawn mower. Hannah's big grey elephant arrived with the fridge. Hannah's mother stood at the front door directing the furniture like a traffic policeman directing cars.

The tall, thin Removal Man, whose name was Joe, carried Hannah's bed up to her new attic bedroom and put it together again with a hammer and pliers from his apron pocket. Hannah watched him.

"You've got a fine view from here," said Joe. "Looking at all those chimney pots of funny shapes and sizes. And that church over there looks like a wedding cake in

tiers. And you must have the
biggest Christmas tree in all the
world."

"It's a Monterey Pine," Hannah
told him. "It's come all the way
from America."

"That's a long way to come,"
said Joe. "Do you know any

American?''

"No," said Hannah. "I only speak English and Willow Tree."

"In America they say 'Hi' instead of 'Hello'," said Joe.

So they both said 'Hi' to the Monterey Pine, but the Monterey Pine said nothing.

"I've got something in my pocket for you," said Joe and he dug in his apron pocket and pulled out a little peg doll.

"It's Looby-Loo!" said Hannah.
"I looked for her everywhere."

"There you are then," said Joe.
"We Removal Men don't leave
anything behind."

"Not even jokes and dreams?"
asked Hannah.

"Certainly not," said Jo. "They
are very carefully packed. You look
under your mattress tonight when
you go to bed."

Then Joe went downstairs and
Hannah's father called her to come
out into the garden again. He was
holding the bag with the rose
cuttings inside. Together they dug
two holes and planted *Ena Harkness*
and *Angela* firmly in the soil.

By the time the Removal Men had unpacked everything it was dark. Hannah went to bed early. She was tired from running up and down the four flights of stairs of Number 325 and from the strangeness of everything. Darjeeling was tired, too. He was curled up on the bottom of Hannah's bed.

Through her window Hannah could see a big office block with a zip of light running down one side of it. The lights in the windows of all the houses of the city were strung across the night like flags, or the bunting Loose End put out on Fair Day. Hannah could see the dark branches of the Monterey Pine lifted to the moon.

And underneath the mattress was Joe's surprise! She wriggled her fingers in close to the bed-springs and found a very small packet. On it was written GLO-STARS. "They're to stick on your ceiling," said her father. "They're luminous — that means they'll shine in the dark just like real stars." Hannah had to stand on the bed to stick the stars on the ceiling. When the light was on you couldn't see them at all, but when Hannah was tucked in under her duvet and the light was switched off, the Glo-Stars glowed and glowed and it was like camping outside under the sky.

"I expect there's lots of dreams in those stars," said Hannah's father as he sat in the darkness on the edge of Hannah's bed. "Look, Darjeeling's dreaming already." Darjeeling's whiskers twitched. (He dreamt of jumping the chimney pots of Totterdown Street and catching the moon.)

"I think I might wake up back in Dungee Farm Cottage," said

Hannah.

"I think you might wake up and unpack some boxes and help me paint the sitting room," said her father. And Hannah laughed because that sounded exciting.

"Good night, Daddy," she said, "and good night, Darjeeling, and good night, Monterey Pine."

But the Monterey Pine said nothing.

# Chapter 4

When Hannah woke up the Glo-Stars had turned back into white sticky stars. Hannah thought they were like Cinderella, back in plain clothes after the ball. Darjeeling had gone for breakfast.

It was a long way from the attic to the kitchen in the basement, but when she got there she had another surprise. Overnight the kitchen had become friendly. The table was in the middle of the room and there was the brown milk jug and the red coffee pot. The kettle was boiling,

the mugs were on the hooks,
Darjeeling's dishes were by the
back door.

Everything — including
Hannah's mother and father — was
looking rather surprised. It was as
if, like the ceiling stars, they had
woken up to find themselves
different.

After breakfast Hannah went out
into the garden to see if *Ena
Harkness*, the scarlet rose, and

*Angela*, the yellow rose, had grown. But they hadn't. Darjeeling followed Hannah outside. He jumped up onto the wall and began walking up and down it as if to say, "This is *my* wall, the wall of *my* new house."

There was another row of houses behind Totterdown Street. The house facing Hannah's garden was painted bright blue and looking out of the first floor windows were two girls, just about Hannah's age. One had red hair and one had yellow hair. The yellow-haired girl popped her head out of one window and the red-haired girl took her head in. Then they did it the other way

round. The red-haired girl popped
her head out and the yellow-haired
girl took her head in. They were
like a cuckoo clock. They were like
the red rose and the yellow rose,
like *Ena Harkness* and *Angela*.

Hannah climbed up onto the wall
to watch them. The two girls saw

her and waved. Then the yellow-
haired girl popped her head out and
said, "Hello!" and the red-haired
girl popped her head out and said,
"Hi!" And Hannah waved and
tried to say, "Hello" and "Hi" in
the right order but the Cuckoo
Clock girls were going too fast.

And as Hannah was saying
"hello-hi-hello-hi-hello-hi" very
fast, like that, she heard a strange
noise behind her. The Monterey
Pine was stirring in the wind. It
rustled all its branches like a
Member of Parliament rustles his
papers before making a Very
Important Speech. But instead of a
big, grand speech, the Monterey

Pine said something surprising. It said, "Coo! Coo!" And again, "Coo! Coo!"

Hannah rushed up the path into the kitchen. "The tree spoke to me!" she cried. "It said, 'Coo, Coo,' just like that. It must be American for 'How are you?' What shall I answer? And I've met the real *Ena Harkness* and *Angela*. They are Cuckoo Clock girls and they live in the house opposite."

"What a very English gabble," said Mr Knap. "Coo, coo, did you say? Sounds like doves to me. Let's go up to your bedroom and look."

So they went up the four flights of stairs to Hannah's attic and looked out of the window at the Monterey Pine. And there, almost at the top of it, they saw what looked like a very roughly made shopping basket, and sitting inside it, two doves.

Down below they could see the Cuckoo Clock girls still popping their heads in and out of the windows of the blue house opposite.

"Coo! Coo!" said the doves.

"I'm very well thank you," said Hannah, in English. "How are you?"

# THE RAINBOW WATCHERS
# Chapter 1

It was a very strange thing, Hannah thought, to be living in the city instead of the country. At night the sky in the city was never really dark and the darkness was never really silent. There was always a low hum in the city's night as if a giant had fallen asleep sucking his thumb and mumbling,

**UM-MUM-UM-MUM-UMMM**
**UM-MUM-UM-MUM-UMMM**

Hannah lived at 325 Totterdown Street. She had been there two days, six hours and seven minutes. They had been a very busy two days, six hours and seven minutes because moving house means a great many boxes to pack and unpack and in the packing and unpacking all your Special Things play hide-and-seek. All the Special Things (like Hannah's pencil box with her name on the lid) had been found now, but Hannah was still homesick for Dungee Farm Cottage in the country where the Knap family had lived for all of Hannah's six years.

Darjeeling was homesick too. Darjeeling was the Knaps' cat. He was black and white and very smart in appearance, looking, with his shiny black coat, white bib and socks, as if he were in evening dress. Darjeeling was so unhappy about moving house that on the first day in 325 Totterdown Street he got into the coal scuttle and tried to pretend he was a lump of coal.

Darjeeling did not like his new cat flap. At Dungee Farm Cottage someone had always opened the kitchen window for him so that he could stalk out like a Very Important Person. Darjeeling thought that wriggling and squeezing your way through a cat flap was undignified. Also, Totterdown Street was full of cats.

City-wise cats. City-slicker cats.
They hid under the cars like lurking
bandits. They raided the dustbins
at night. And each Totterdown
Street cat had its very own window-
sill. To Darjeeling, who was used to
streaking silently (and alone) across
dark country fields, they seemed like
a fierce Gang.

Darjeeling felt lost and shy and uncomfortable in Totterdown Street and so did Hannah. She felt lost and little in the big busyness of the city. She felt shy of the other children in the street who, on a Sunday morning, marched up and down with bright coloured buckets and sponges, washing cars for fifty pence a time. And she felt as uncomfortable in the new house as in a new dress that was still shop-stiff and didn't fit her shape properly.

If it hadn't been for the Cuckoo Clock girls, Eliza and Jenny, Hannah would have been very miserable indeed.

The Cuckoo Clock girls lived in the house that faced Hannah's back garden. It was a bright blue house as if someone who wanted to remember holiday-blue sky and holiday-blue sea had painted it that colour. It was Hannah's father who had nicknamed Eliza and Jenny the Cuckoo Clock girls when he saw them, one at each window of the blue house, popping their heads in and out and saying, "Hello! Hi! Hello! Hi!" like a pair of cuckoos popping out to tell the time. Hannah hoped that Eliza and Jenny might become her friends but she thought they might not because, after all, they had each other.

On the second day in the new
house there was no sign of the
Cuckoo Clock girls and on the third
day it was raining. Hannah's father
had gone back to work and
Hannah's mother said she was tired
out. She was going to have an
afternoon nap.

"A nap for Mrs Knap," said
Hannah and they both laughed.
But Hannah didn't really feel like

laughing. She felt sad. City rain was different from country rain. It didn't smell so sweet and instead of making the fields greener it made the pavements dirtier.

Hannah went up to her attic bedroom to see if, perhaps, the Cuckoo Clock girls were at their windows so that she could wave to them. But they weren't. They were outside . . . doing something rather odd.

The Cuckoo Clock girls were sitting on the wall in front of the bright blue house. They sat there in the pouring rain, not talking at all but just staring up into the sky as if they were expecting an angel or a flying ice-cream van. Eliza held a big striped umbrella which she twirled now and again and Jenny wore yellow wellingtons and kicked her legs up and down against the wall.

Hannah was very curious. She went downstairs, found her own wellingtons (blue) and a mac she had almost-but-not-quite grown out of and she went out of the kitchen door and down to the bottom of the garden. The Cuckoo Clock girls smiled and waved at Hannah and then carried on looking up at the sky as if they didn't want to miss whatever it was they were looking for.

Hannah felt rather silly standing

there in the rain. Eliza and Jenny
had that 'do not disturb' look which
Mr Knap sometimes wore when he
was adding up his bills. Hannah
looked up at the sky too, but it all
looked city-grey to her although the
rain was lighter and the clouds were
moving away like a bad temper
turning into a good one.

Hannah's hair was getting very

wet and the rain was plopping
down her neck where the mac didn't
fit. She looked up and down the
street to see if there was a circus
coming or a band but there was
nothing and nobody, only the cars
whooshing along in the rain.
Hannah counted twenty-two cars
and then she called across the road
to Eliza and Jenny.

"What are you looking for?"

"Rainbows," said Eliza, not
taking her eyes off the sky. "We're
the Rainbow Watchers," and she
twirled the striped umbrella.

"It's our job," said Jenny.

"We get paid for it," said Eliza
importantly.

"I don't believe you," said
Hannah. "Lots of people look at
rainbows but nobody gets *paid* for
it."

"*We* do!" said Jenny. "Mrs
Middlesome-Merry pays us.
Whenever we see a rainbow we
have to run up the road and tell
her."

"She lives up there," said Eliza,

pointing to the top of the street. Totterdown Street was on a hill and Hannah's house and the blue house were half-way up the hill. Mrs Middlesome-Merry lived at the very top.

"Is she a bit mad?" asked Hannah as politely as she could.

"She's a painter," said Jenny, "and she says she takes colour lessons from the rainbow."

"She says there's an unknown colour," said Eliza, "and that if you look long enough at violet and have very special eyes, you might see it."

"She pays us seven pence a rainbow," said Jenny.

"What an awkward number," said Hannah.

"It is rather," agreed Eliza, "it makes three and a half pence each, but you see it's one pence for every colour of the rainbow and there are seven colours."

Jenny sang,

*"One pence for jolly red, one pence for blue,"*

*"One pence for grassy green and one for orange, too.*

*One pence violet-oh, one pence for yellow,*

*And here-we-go with indigo*

*It's seven pence a rainy-bow!"*

Jenny's yellow wellies beat the wall in time to the song and Eliza

twirled the umbrella.

"Would you get eight pence if
you saw the unknown colour?"
asked Hannah.

"I suppose we might," said
Jenny. "But we never will. You've
got to have Super-Natural eyes,"
and Jenny made her right eye cross
with her left eye.

"Why can't Mrs Muddlesome
look for her own rainbow?" asked
Hannah.

"Mrs Middlesome-Merry," corrected Eliza. "And she can't watch for rainbows because she's got seven big sons ..."

"Like the seven colours ..." put in Jenny.

"And they eat and eat and eat," said Eliza, "so she's too busy making soup and stew to go looking for rainbows."

The rain had almost stopped now and the sun was just beginning to move out from behind the clouds. Both Eliza and Jenny stopped talking and stared up at the sky again.

Hannah left them to it and went indoors. From her attic bedroom she watched the rainbow rising up over the city, fresh and country-clean. Eliza and Jenny jumped off the wall and went running up the street to Mrs Middlesome-Merry's.

Darjeeling had come out of the coal bucket and was curled up on Hannah's bed. Hannah tickled him behind his ears. "Oh, Darjeeling," she said, "I wish I could be a Rainbow Watcher."

But Darjeeling only twitched his whiskers. He was having a nightmare about The Gang.

# Chapter 2

It rained all week. "April showers," said Mrs Knap, unpegging the washing from the line.

Eliza and Jenny were in and out of the blue house like a pair of over-worked cuckoos. In just seven days there were three rainbows. This meant, Hannah worked out, that Eliza and Jenny had made twenty-one pence between them, or eleven and a half pence each.

But on Friday afternoon it was dry and Eliza and Jenny came for tea. They looked all over 325

Totterdown Street and Hannah had
to draw her bedroom curtains so
that they could see the Glo-Stars
which Joe the removal man had
given her to stick on her ceiling.
The Glo-Stars shone in the night so
that Hannah felt she was sleeping
under the sky.

"Can we come and stay the
night?" Eliza wanted to know.

"Then we can star-gaze by night
and rainbow-watch by day," said
Jenny.

"Tell me about Mrs Middlesome-
Merry," said Hannah.

"She cooks buckets of soup and
paints dozens of paintings," said
Eliza.

"She's all over soup splodges and paint splodges," said Jenny.

"With a violet blob on her nose," said Eliza.

"She has violet everywhere!" said Jenny. "A violet bath sponge and a violet telephone and a violet hat for Sundays."

"But she makes lovely pictures," said Eliza after a pause in which they had all sat imagining violet everything. Darjeeling, lying on Hannah's bed again, rose, arched his back and leapt neatly into Hannah's lap as if quite certain that black and white, his colours, were the very best.

"Mrs Middlesome-Merry paints

flowers," said Jenny. "Flowers and flowers and nothing but flowers. And every painting has a little bit of violet in it."

"Mrs Middlesome-Merry says a painting should be like a lamp in your room," said Eliza.

But Hannah had stopped listening. She was thinking of flowers and flowers and nothing but flowers; of the fields near Dungee Farm Cottage full of buttercups and of the place in the woods called the Bluebell Glade. Hannah's eyes felt dull and dusty in the city as if they needed something to drink like the yellow of buttercups and the blue of bluebells.

It began to rain then and Eliza and Jenny jumped up and said they must go. They had work to do. Rainbow Watching.

Hannah wandered down to the kitchen where her mother was moving things around again, carrying a rocking chair from one corner of the room to another and then back again.

"I can't seem to settle," said Hannah's mother. "Sometimes I feel all at odds with myself, like Darjeeling."

"Maybe you should sit in the coal bucket instead of the rocking chair," said Hannah.

Mrs Knap laughed and looked

about the kitchen again. "What we need," she said, "is some potted plants and... and some pictures on the wall."

"Mrs Middlesome-Merry!" cried Hannah.

"Mrs Who?"

"Mrs Middlesome-Merry," said Hannah, "she's a painter and she lives at the top of the street and she paints flowers and flowers and nothing but flowers. She uses rainbow colours, only violet's her favourite and she thinks there's an unknown colour that nobody's seen."

"An unknown colour?" said Hannah's mother. "What could it be? Well, all the known colours are quite good enough for me."

"Can we go and buy a painting?" asked Hannah. "One with all the known colours, the colours of the rainbow in it?"

"We cannot," said Hannah's mother. "I want you to help me move the sofa in the sitting room. It's in the wrong place." So they went into the sitting room and Hannah tried to lift one end of the sofa and her mother tried to lift the other and Darjeeling, who happened to be sleeping in the middle, got very huffy and went off back into the coal scuttle. But they couldn't lift the sofa at all, it was too heavy.

Hannah's mother got very red in

the face and cross and said they'd
have to leave the sofa until
Hannah's father got home and she
went off into the kitchen to make
the supper in a rather angry-
banging way.

Hannah went back up to her attic
and watched the rain polishing the
roofs. Then she got out her crayons
and did one picture of buttercups
and another of bluebells and stuck
them on the wall so that the wall
began to look like the field near
Dungee Farm Cottage. Only the
yellow wasn't *quite* as yellow as
buttercups and the blue not *quite* as
blue as bluebells.

But when Mr Knap came home,

Hannah forgot about missing the country fields and Mrs Knap forgot about moving the sofa because Mr Knap carried a large square parcel very carefully wrapped in layers and layers of newspaper.

There was so much newspaper round the parcel that Hannah said they ought to play Pass the Parcel, but Mr Knap said no, he was going to unwrap it and he did. When the last piece of newspaper came off Hannah saw . . . a picture. A very cheerful picture of bright red tulips in a big brown jug.

"The very thing!" cried Mrs Knap. "I knew something was missing from this house. It was tulips!" But Hannah was looking at the name, written in squiggly paint-writing in the corner of the picture. She could make out two large M's.

"It's by Sybil Middlesome-Merry," said her father. "I saw it in a shop window this afternoon and I thought, My! You could warm your hands in front of those tulips! And then I thought, Our house needs warming up. I'll buy us

a house-warming present. So I did
and here it is!"

"Daddy, it's a painting by the
Rainbow Lady!" cried Hannah
jumping up and down. "She lives at
the top of our street and Eliza and
Jenny watch rainbows for her and
oh, I wish I could too!"

"Well I never!" said Mr Knap.

"Fancy a painter living in our street."

"Red is my very favourite colour," said Mrs Knap. "They warm the cockles of my heart, those tulips," and she gave Mr Knap a big kiss and went off into the kitchen to do something happy-and-clattery (which turned out to be cottage pie) with a lot of saucepans.

But Hannah sat on the floor and looked at the painting propped up on the unmoved sofa and she thought that the tulips warmed your hands and warmed your cockles and warmed your whole self. They warmed the house, too. They made 325 Totterdown Street feel like home.

# Chapter 3

"Rain before seven, fine before eleven," said Mr Knap.

It was Saturday and raining again. Eliza and Jenny were out early, sitting on the wall in the rain and drinking breakfast mugs of tea.

"Those cuckoos will turn into ducks," said Hannah's father. Mr Knap was wandering all over the house trying to find just the right place to hang Mrs Middlesome-Merry's tulips. He tried them in the sitting room, he tried them in the hall, he tried them in the kitchen –

he tried almost every wall. Mr
Knap knocked a lot of nails in a lot
of walls and Ooohed and Aaahed
over the tulips for so long that Mrs
Knap, in a voice snappy as a
snapdragon, said, "What about the
Saturday shopping?"

"The trouble is," said Hannah's
father, "that I'd really like the
tulips in *every* room." Then he put
down the painting and his hammer
and nails and he put on his jacket
and said to Hannah, "Come on –
let's go up the street and say hello
to Mrs Middlesome-Merry and tell
her how much we like her tulips."

So Hannah and her father set
off up the street to number 221

Totterdown Street which was where
Mrs Middlesome-Merry lived. On
the way they met Eliza and Jenny.
Jenny had two red bows in her hair
and Eliza wore a rainbow-striped
cap and, when they heard where
Hannah and her father were going,
they asked if they could come, too,
and Mr Knap said they could.

It was as if Mrs Middlesome-Merry had chosen number 221 Totterdown Street so as to be as near to rainbows as possible. It was a tall house, like Hannah's, but on every window-sill there was a cat and a window-box full of trailing geraniums or tumbling nasturtiums. Outside the front door was a big tub full of violet pansies.

Hannah half-expected Mrs Middlesome-Merry to look like a flower herself and to be wearing her violet hat, but when the door opened Hannah saw a small chubby woman with yellow-going-grey hair and bluebell-blue eyes. She wore a big apron splodged with

paint colours and soup colours and
the pocket of her apron was full of
paintbrushes and soup ladles.

"Good morning," said Hannah's
father, "my name is Thomas Knap
and this is my daughter, Hannah.
We live just down the street at

number 325 and yesterday I bought one of your paintings – *Red Tulips*."

"Oh, how very nice!" said Mrs Middlesome-Merry turning red as the tulips. "I do like to know that a painting has got a good home. Is it a good home?" she asked. Hannah laughed because Mrs Middlesome-Merry made a painting sound like a kitten or a puppy but Eliza and Jenny said as loudly as they could, "Oh yes, it *is* a good home."

"Then come and see my other paintings," said Mrs Middlesome-Merry. "I have a studio at the top of the house, in the attic."

"Like my bedroom," said Hannah.

"Then you're very lucky," said Mrs Middlesome-Merry. "Always get as near to the sky as you can. Good for the health. And you might get a glimpse through."

"A glimpse through to what?" asked Hannah, thinking of the sky suddenly opening up so that you could look inside and see God having His breakfast or maybe His tea. But Mrs Middlesome-Merry only laughed and began climbing the stairs. From the kitchen there was a strong smell of onion soup.

Climbing up to the studio was not easy for Hannah and her father because at the bottom of the stairs was a big brass tub and in the tub an ivy began; and the ivy went on and on, in and out of the banister rails in great loops and swirls, knots and jungle tangles as though it were trying to take over the whole house.

When they reached Mrs Middlesome-Merry's attic they found that it was more like a garden than an attic. The room had a large skylight and beneath it a big wooden table. On the table were pots and pots of flowers – hyacinths in bowls, sweet-peas in jugs, dog-daisies in milk bottles, lilies in a jam jar, poppies in a yoghurt pot. And all round the walls were paintings of flowers –

snowdrops and roses, dahlias and dizzy-lizzies, daffodils and delphiniums.

Hannah let her eyes have a very good drink and then she said, "I feel as if I'm back in the country in here."

"I'd like to buy a painting for every room of the house," said Hannah's father, "but I'm afraid I can't afford it."

"You'll have to start painting your own," said Mrs Middlesome-Merry, "but here you are – these will cheer things up." And she gave Mr Knap a pot of trailing geraniums, Hannah the yoghurt pot of poppies, Eliza the milk bottle of dog-daisies and Jenny the jam jar of lilies.

"Have you ever seen the unknown colour?" asked Hannah because she simply *had* to ask.

"Oh no!" said Mrs Middlesome-Merry. "The unknown colour's a mystery. That's why I like it. Soup and mystery are the things I like best in all the world." Then suddenly Mrs Middlesome-Merry stood very still and sniffed. "My soup!" she cried. "My onion soup! It's bubbling over like joy!" And they all had to hurry downstairs again and Eliza and Jenny reached the kitchen first because they were used to jumping over the ivy knots.

They were just in time to save most
of the soup.

"Really I'd like my kitchen to be
in the attic, too," said Mrs
Middlesome-Merry. "It would save
all this running up and down and I
could cook in sunlight and twilight
and rainbow light..." She had
pulled out a paintbrush and was

just about to stir the soup with it
when Hannah called out, "Stop!
Stop! Mrs Muddlesome, that's a
paintbrush not a soup ladle!" And
Mrs Middlesome-Merry looked
down at her hand and laughed.
"Oh dear," she said, "they nearly
had violet soup! Eliza and Jenny, I
think you've found a very clever
friend in Hannah."

"Maybe she could be a Rainbow

Watcher with us," said Eliza.

"Three is a much nicer number than two," said Jenny.

And Hannah held her breath and Mrs Middlesome-Merry said, "It is, isn't it? Would you like to be a Rainbow Watcher, Hannah? My rates of pay are seven pence a rainbow. Would that suit?"

"Oh yes!" said Hannah. "That would suit very nicely indeed thank you!"

"Let's shake on it then," said Mrs Middlesome-Merry. So they all shook hands because no-one wanted to be left out and it was a rather onion-soup sort of handshake but they were all too polite to say so.

After that they went back down Totterdown Street. They looked very much like a moving garden, Hannah's father carrying the trailing geraniums, Hannah the yoghurt pot of poppies, Eliza the milk bottle of dog-daisies and Jenny the jam jar of lilies.

And when they reached 325 Totterdown Street there was Darjeeling waiting for them. He had discovered his very own window-sill.

"Well, well," said Hannah's father. "I think Darjeeling's joined The Gang."

"And I've joined the Rainbow Watchers," said Hannah happily.

# MORE WALKER PAPERBACKS
## For You to Enjoy

☐ 0-7445-2306-0    *Midnight Feast*    £2.99
by Hannah Cole

☐ 0-7445-2313-3    *The Dream Camel and the Dazzling Cat*    £2.99
by Diana Hendry

☐ 0-7445-2314-1    *Fay Cow and the Honey Machine*    £2.99
by Peter Hunt

☐ 0-7445-2302-8    *Smudge*    £2.99
by Alison Morgan

☐ 0-7445-1706-0    *The Russian Doll*    £2.99
by Joan Smith

☐ 0-7445-2300-1    *Imran's Secret*    £2.99
by Nadya Smith

☐ 0-7445-1462-2    *Will You Come on Wednesday?*    £2.99
by Nadya Smith

**Walker Paperbacks are available from most booksellers. They are also available by post: just tick the titles you want, fill in the form below and send it to Walker Books Ltd, PO Box 11, Falmouth, Cornwall TR10 9EN.**

Please send a cheque or postal order and allow the following for postage and packing:
UK and BFPO Customers – £1.00 for first book, plus 50p for the second book and plus 30p for each additional book to a maximum charge of £3.00.
Overseas and Eire Customers – £2.00 for first book, plus £1.00 for the second book and plus 50p per copy for each additional book.
Prices are correct at time of going to press, but are subject to change without notice.

Name _____

Address _____

_____